THE STORY OF DOCTOR DOLITTLE

by HUGH LOFTING

#2 The Circus Crocodile

Adapted by Diane Namm

Illustrated by John Kanzler

Sterling Publishing Co., Inc.
New York

Library of Congress Cataloging-in-Publication Data Available

10   9   8   7   6   5   4

Published by Sterling Publishing Co., Inc.
387 Park Avenue South, New York, NY 10016
Copyright © 2006 by Barnes and Noble, Inc.
Illustrations © 2006 by John Kanzler
Distributed in Canada by Sterling Publishing
^{c}/o Canadian Manda Group, 165 Dufferin Street
Toronto, Ontario, Canada M6K 3H6
Distributed in the United Kingdom by GMC Distribution Services
Castle Place, 166 High Street, Lewes, East Sussex, England BN7 1XU
Distributed in Australia by Capricorn Link (Australia) Pty. Ltd.
P.O. Box 704, Windsor, NSW 2756, Australia

Printed in China 12/09

Sterling ISBN 13: 978 1-4027-3292-8
        ISBN 10: 1-4027-3292-9

For information about custom editions, special sales, premium and
corporate purchases, please contact Sterling Special Sales
Department at 800-805-5489 or specialsales@sterlingpub.com.

Contents

The Circus Comes to Town

It was a big day in Puddleby.
The circus had come to town!
Everyone was enjoying
the show—everyone
but the crocodile.
He was thinking,
"My mouth hurts!"

He heard about Doctor Dolittle
from other animals
and ran away to find him.

"Open wide," said Doctor Dolittle
to the poor crocodile.
So he did.

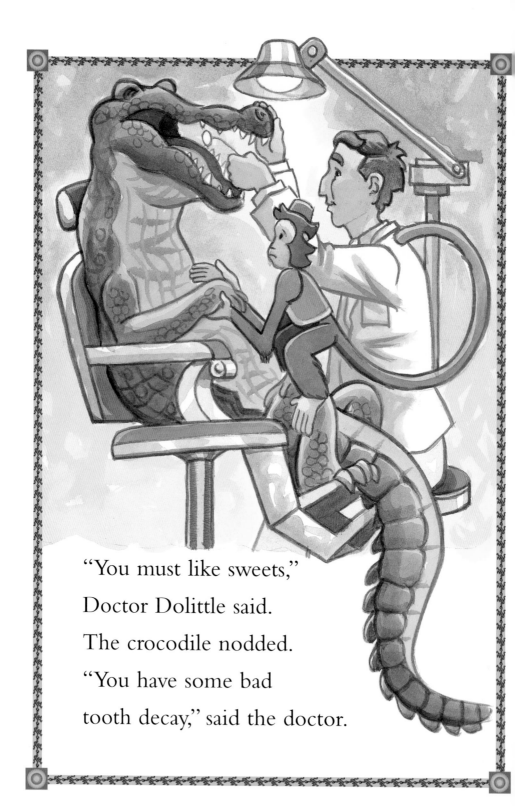

"You must like sweets,"
Doctor Dolittle said.
The crocodile nodded.
"You have some bad
tooth decay," said the doctor.

Very, very carefully,
Doctor Dolittle put fillings
in the crocodile's teeth.

The animals brought
the crocodile balloons
to help him feel better.
Soon, he did.

The ringmaster came
to Doctor Dolittle's house
to get the crocodile,
but he didn't want
to go back.

The circus left that very day,
but the crocodile stayed behind.

"Don't worry," the doctor said.

"We have plenty of room here!"

No, Thank You

After the circus left,
the crocodile was sad.
Doctor Dolittle talked to
the other animals about it.
"We will try to make him feel at
home," they said, and they tried.

"Do you want to play a game?"
Chee-Chee asked him.
"No, thank you," the crocodile said.

"Do you want to play catch?"
asked Jip the dog.
"No, thank you,"
the crocodile said.

"Do you want to swim with me?"
asked Dab-Dab the duck.
"No, thank you,"
the crocodile said.

"Do you want to roll in the mud?"
asked Gub-Gub the pig.
"No, thank you,"
the crocodile said.

"Do you want to eat a banana?"
asked Polynesia the parrot.
"That always makes
Chee-Chee happy!"
"No, thank you,"
the crocodile said.

The animals were worried.
"We have tried everything,"
they told Doctor Dolittle,
"but the crocodile will not smile!"

Doctor Dolittle thought
and thought and thought,
but he could not think
what to do, until . . .

. . . the crocodile burst
into the room and said,
"I am sad because
I want to go home!"
"To the circus?"
asked the doctor.
"No, to Africa," he said.

Packing Up

That night, the doctor and
the animals came up with a plan.
They would take
the crocodile back
where he wanted to be—
back to his home across the sea.
They went to pack their bags.

Chee-Chee the monkey
packed bananas.

Jip the dog
packed bones.

Dab-Dab the duck
packed water.

Gub-Gub the pig
packed mud.

Polynesia the parrot
packed birdseed.

Doctor Dolittle
packed
everything else.

"This is very nice of you,"
said the crocodile,
"but my home is far away.
It is too far to walk there."

Doctor Dolittle smiled.

"Leave it to me!" he said.

The Big Good-bye

The animals followed the doctor
through the dark and sleepy town.
The crocodile still did not smile.
He still was not sure
he would ever get home.
Then the doctor stopped.
He pointed at something.
"Surprise!" he said.

"What is it?" asked Chee-Chee.

"It is our ship," the doctor said.

"Will it sail?" asked the crocodile.

"Indeed," the doctor said.

Just then, the people
of Puddleby arrived.
"We could not let you leave
without saying good-bye,"
they said to the doctor
and his friends.

"What is all this?"
asked Doctor Dolittle.

"Presents," the people said.

"How nice!" said the doctor.

"Thank you very much!"

After he hugged them all,
Doctor Dolittle said it was time to leave.
He got on the ship. "All aboard!"
he called. The animals got on, too.

"Good-bye, good-bye!"
the people called out.
The doctor and the animals
waved back at them.
"Good-bye!" they said . . .

. . . except the crocodile.

He said nothing at all.

He just smiled!